GARVEY IN THE DARK

NIKKI GRIMES

GARVEY *IN THE* DARK

WORDSONG

AN IMPRINT OF ASTRA BOOKS FOR YOUNG READERS

New York

Wordsong
An imprint of Astra Books for Young Readers,
a division of Astra Publishing House
astrapublishinghouse.com
Printed in the United States of America

Library of Congress Cataloging-in-Publication Data

Names: Grimes, Nikki, author.
Title: Garvey in the dark / Nikki Grimes.
Description: First edition. | New York : Wordsong, 2022. | Audience: Ages
  8-12. | Audience: Grades 4-6. | Summary: "Capturing the shock and
  reverberations of the COVID-19 pandemic through poetry, as Garvey's life
  goes into lockdown and his father becomes sick, Garvey must find a way
  to use his newfound musical skills to bring hope to both his father and
  himself"– Provided by publisher.
Identifiers: LCCN 2022024229 (print) | LCCN 2022024230 (ebook) | ISBN
  9781635925265 (hardcover) | ISBN 9781635925456 (epub)
Subjects: LCSH: Children's poetry, American. | CYAC: COVID-19 Pandemic,
  2020—Poetry. | American poetry. | LCGFT: Poetry.
Classification: LCC PS3557.R489982 G37 2022 (print) | LCC PS3557.R489982
  (ebook) | DDC 811/.6–dc23/eng/20220526
LC record available at https://lccn.loc.gov/2022024229
LC ebook record available at https://lccn.loc.gov/2022024230

First edition

10 9 8 7 6 5 4 3 2 1

Design by Barbara Grzeslo
The text is set in Bembo.
The titles are set in Active One.

For Lucie Malskeit, the niece of my heart

Contents

Garvey's California COVID-19 Timeline 2020

How COVID Unfolds in Garvey's Southern California World

Garvey lives in a Southern California suburb. Though no athlete, he lives in a climate where he can be outdoors in his backyard as much as he chooses.

January 25, 2020—First case of COVID-19 in California.

February 2—The first person-to-person transmission of the virus in the state is discovered. Statewide cases rise to six.

February 3—Santa Clara, CA, is the first county to declare a local health emergency.

February 5—350 Americans from two international flights are quarantined on military bases for two weeks.

February 14—San Diego County declares a local health emergency. Two county citizens test positive for COVID.

February 16—Passengers from the Diamond Princess Cruise Ship, who are quarantined in northern California, test positive for coronavirus.

February 25—San Francisco's mayor calls the virus an emergency.

February 27—The state monitors at least 8,400 people as the California case count rises.

February 29—California K–12 school and college leadership prepare for possible distance learning.

March 4—Governor Newsom declares a state emergency.

March 7—San Francisco bans large gatherings.

March 11—Governor tightens gathering restrictions statewide as The World Health Organization declares COVID-19 a pandemic.

March 13—Schools across the state close due to COVID.

Shortly after midnight, Breonna Taylor is wrongfully killed by police in Louisville, KY. Reverberations reach California.

March 19—A statewide shelter-in-place order is issued.

March 21—The state leases two hospitals to increase the number of hospital beds available.

March 24—A 17-year-old in Los Angeles County dies of COVID-19.

March 31—California schools likely will be closed for the remainder of the academic year.

April 14—Newsom charts a path to reopening California.

April 30—California beach closures are announced.

May 1—2,500+ people rally in Huntington Beach, CA, to protest beach closures.

May 8—Newsom says Californians will vote by mail.

May 10—Mother's Day service in Mendocino County church leads to COVID outbreak.

May 13—Los Angeles County beaches reopen—with restrictions.

May 20—1,200 pastors vow to resume in-person services.

May 21—Sheriff arrests shelter-in-place protesters at a San Clemente pier.

May 24—More COVID cases are linked to Mendocino County church gathering.

May 25—George Floyd, Jr. is murdered by a Minneapolis police officer who kneeled on his neck for nine minutes, ignoring Floyd's pleas to breathe.

May 28—The school year ends in Riverside County and COVID deaths in the US pass the 100,000 mark.

May 30—After record-setting temperatures, health officials worry that effects of the pandemic will exacerbate annual heat-wave dangers.

June 8—California State education officials announce recommendations for a return to in-school teaching in the fall.

June 12—Restaurants, retail stores, bars, gyms, and religious services are okayed to reopen.

June 14—A hospitalization record is set over the weekend.

June 18—Californians are ordered to wear masks in public.

June 24—More records are set as COVID-19 cases continue to rise.

July 17—Newsom's strict safety requirements for the new school year mean that most children will be distance learning.

GARVEY IN THE DARK

Prologue

Different. The same. . . .
*That's my answer if you ask
how I am after
The Invisible Beast broke
into our house, and our world.*

Garvey

I ride the ripples
of song. That may sound silly
but singing heals my
heart. And in a way, music
gave me the dad I needed.

ANGIE

Sometimes I wonder
how Angie and I came from
the same family.
She's a long-legged jock. Me?
Short, squat bookworm. Go figure.

THE MYSTERY OF GENES

Mom is half Angie,
half me. Mom and I play chess
when we're not reading,
but she's quick to kick any
ball Sis or Dad toss her way.

On the other hand,
Dad's all sports, all the time. Well,
almost. Luckily
his vocabulary does
include music, just like mine.

I guess it all works.
Every family has its quirks,
right? Ours could be worse.
But here's the main thing: true love
shows up when we're together.

SUBURBAN MORNING

Taps on my window
let me know Joe is ready
for our daily game
of catch. You'd think we'd get bored,
except baseball's how we speak

without using words.
Who cares that I'm no athlete?
I grab my mitt, meet
my friend, take my stance. "Let's go,"
is all we say. Then we play.

MANNY FOR SHORT

Funny how time helps
you dive beneath the surface
when it comes to friends.
I hardly notice Manny's
pink eyes or colorless skin

or his snow-white hair.
He's just Emmanuel, or
Manny for short, the
other tenor from chorus
who sings in the key of we.

JANUARY REPORTS OF A MYSTERY ILLNESS

One Sunday, at lunch,
Dad mentions something awful
happening over
there, somewhere far away, but
I'm only half listening.

It's not like we go
out for pizza every day.
Don't ask me to pay
attention when melty cheese,
thin-crust goodness is calling!

WEEK-NIGHT LESSON

Dad's fingers on mine,
he shows me the way to play.
My new guitar is
quickly becoming a friend
and, finally, so is Dad.

CHECKMATE

Mom and I play chess
one Sunday and Dad walks in
as I swipe Mom's queen.
"Checkmate!" I belt out. "Take that!"
Mom falls back in her chair as

if I just hit her.
"Ugh! I didn't see that one
coming. Well, guess I'll
get the ratatouille on."
(Manny taught me what that is!)

I notice Dad's eyes
are still glued to the chessboard.
"I don't get this game,"
he says. I shrug, wondering
how to explain. "Uhh, would you

like me to teach you?"
I hold my breath. "Hmmm. Okay,"
Dad says, sitting down.
"Where do we start?" *Concentrate,*
I tell myself. *Quit grinning.*

OH, WELL

Three tries, and this New
York transplant decides chess is
not for him. Okay.
At least he gave it a shot.
Now it's my turn, which is why

I'm munching on chips
and dip next to Dad, watching
Monday Night Football.
So what if I don't get it?
Dad and I are together.

FEBRUARY WHISPERS

I walk in on Mom
and Dad discussing planeloads
of Americans
in quarantine nearby. Their
voices drop to whispers the

minute they see me.
"Who died?" I ask, curious.
"No one died here, Son,"
says Dad, shooting a message
to Mom with his eyes. I shrug

and sleepwalk to the
kitchen like a puppet on
a mission. I let
my growling belly pull the
strings, then—*Yes! One cookie left*.

Spring Break Countdown

February, and
I'm ready to roll winter
up like a carpet
and pack it away. Spring break,
hurry! Please! Don't make me beg.

BREAKING NEWS

I overhear two
teachers in the school hall. One
says, "San Francisco
just declared a virus e—
Garvey, don't be late to class."

I pick up the pace,
squirreling away bits of—
what? Conversation?
News? Something here reminds me
of my parents, whispering

weeks ago. Lately,
their voices are getting—I
don't know—a little
tighter? It's probably my
imagination. That's all.

Easter Prep

I've been singing in
my school chorus for a while,
and since I started,
Pastor's been pestering me
to join choir. But I'm busy.

There's no running from
Pastor, though, when he asks me
to sing a solo
for Easter. "I heard about
that solo you did with that

chorus of yours, young
man." "Garvey would be glad to,"
Dad answers for me.
Great! No getting out of it
now. But what if I mess up?

In church? In front of
God? I swear, Mom can read my
mind. She comes close and
softly says, "You'll be fine, Son.
Just open your mouth and sing."

"Okay, Pastor Mike,"
I say. But by the end of
the day, I'm sweating.
pls pls pls, I text Manny,
asking him to go to church

with me. It's March, so
Easter won't be here for weeks,
but still, just thinking
about it makes me nervous.
Manny usually goes

to the Catholic Mass
with his grandma, but I hope
this one time, Manny
will (please!) go to church with me.
chill, texts Manny, *ibt*.

FIST BUMP

I fist bump Manny
when I see him the next day.
He smiles that easy
way that says *Dude, I got you.*
It's not even a question.

GIRLFRIEND

"Joe and Deondra,
sitting in a tree," I sing,
teasing Joe about
this girl he likes at school. "Oh,
grow up!" he says. Even so,

we're both laughing. "K–
i–s–s–i–n–g." "Quit!"
says Joe. "Fine!" I say
then throw my hands up, humming.
Joe play-punches me. And grins.

Average Afternoon

"Mom, can you help me?
This algebra problem makes
no sense," I grumble.
"I'm getting dinner. Angie?
Help your brother." "Can't!" she says.

"I've got volleyball,
remember? Sorry, Garvey."
Whatever. Angie's
always too busy for me.
Guess I'm on my own. Surprise!

LATE FOR DINNER

Stomach empty, I
fly upstairs, determined to
crack pre-algebra
before I sit down to eat.
I have to beat this problem!

In the Novel I'm Reading

Ten o'clock at night
Emmett Till fights to make me
understand how not
to become a ghost like him,
how to keep walking this earth.

I'll try, I whisper
just as my eyes flutter shut.
But behind the lids
Black boy ghosts rise, the bullets
that pierced them, pounded to dust.

THE MORNING AFTER

I wake up too late
to toss balls with Joe. *sry*,
I text him, then throw
on stale clothes and race to school
for another boring day.

Friday the 13th

The principal makes
the PA system crackle
so late in the day,
hardly anyone listens
except the teacher and me.

"ATTENTION: Staff, there
will be an emergency
meeting once students
are dismissed. Please make your way
to the auditorium."

What's that all about?
I wonder. But my question
gets drowned out by the
sudden sound of rain pounding
the rooftop. *Oh, great,* I think.

*Wish I didn't live
close enough to walk home. Sheesh!*
The last bell rings and the hall
looks like a track meet, all those
feet flying for the front door

except mine. They aim
straight for the school library.
*Please, please have Book Two
of The Lost Tribes. I need it.*
Miss Thompson opens the door.

"Garvey! We're closed, but—
come in. Quick! Now, what can I
get for you?" Three books
and one borrowed umbrella
later, I head home, happy.

Heavy Load

Mom muscles her way
through our front door, with a box
heavy as iron.
Textbooks, markers, and posters
elbow each other for room.

Balancing on top:
Mom's document camera.
Whoa! "Mom, what's the deal?
Were you fired, or did you quit?"
That's when Sis bounces in. "Hey!"

Mom huffs. "Would someone
please give me a hand? Today?"
I reach for the box.
Sis grabs the camera and
Mom blurts out, "The schools are closed."

"For the weekend," Sis
and I say in unison.
Mom shakes her head, no.
"Our district is closed until
sometime after the spring break.

Angie and I squeal.
"Two weeks' vacation! Great news!"
"Well, not exactly . . ."
Mom says, her voice trailing off.
"Though I guess it is—for you."

Too happy to ask
what Mom means, I race upstairs,
blow through my homework,
then—finally—slip inside
The Lost Tribes: Safe Harbor. Ahh!

Varsity Blues

By dinner, Angie's
lips pucker, sour as lemons.
"What's wrong?" I whisper.
She shrugs. "My soccer team's end-
of-season matches may be

cancelled. We don't know."
"Oh." What can I say? I turn
to Mom. "Won't Angie's
soccer meets be rescheduled?"
"They're *matches*, and I don't know,"

she says, staring straight
at Sis. "Let's wait and see." Our
least favorite words.
I reach under the table
and squeeze Angie's hand. "Sorry."

SECRETS

Dad gets home late, joins
Mom inches from the TV
studying the news
like they're cramming for a test.
Their whispers make me nervous

though I can't say why.
I finish my turn clearing
the table and load
the dishwasher quiet as
a ninja, but still can't hear

what they're saying. I
shrug, thinking *It's probably*
not interesting,
anyway. Besides, I've got
that new book waiting. "Good night!"

BREONNA TAYLOR

Saturday serves up
news that annihilates my
appetite. One more
Black person killed by police
the night before. Who can eat?

I hit the shower,
try to hold back the rage and
the fear that I could
be next. Can't dwell on that, though.
So I grab my mitt and go.

Compared to What

Later, I catch Mom
crying in the kitchen. I
look for onions, but
don't see one. "Mom?" "Sorry, Son,"
she says, grabbing a tissue.

"I was just thinking
about students on breakfast
and free lunch programs.
How will they eat with schools closed?"
I never thought about that.

I never had to.
Mom sees me bite my lip. "It's
okay, Garvey. We
teachers will figure something
out, somehow. It's what we do."

Mom manages the
shadow of a smile so I'll
believe her like I
need to. What else can I do?
God, I hope you're listening.

SUNDAY CINEMA

After church, Mom drives
Joe, Manny, and me cross town
to see a movie—
something PG, of course. Duh!
(Mom thinks we're babies.) Turns out

it wasn't half bad—
though nowhere near as good as
comic book movies.
The new one hit the screen two
days ago. But who's counting?

TAKE A BREAK, MOM

Poor Mom spends the week
married to the telephone
talking with parents,
reading emails from school, and
making lesson plans—that is

when she's not in some
webinar learning how to
teach online. I don't
know why she's bothering. School
won't be closed that long, will it?

FREE HOLIDAY

Vacation Part Two
starts in a few days: spring break!
I bet after that
schools will be open again.
Angie says she's not so sure.

"This new virus—it's
bad, Garvey, and now it's here
in California.
People are getting sick and
dying, and—it's just real bad."

Angie's words are stirred
with fear and I can feel them
burn for a moment.
Then, the pain passes, and I
tell myself Sis must be wrong.

At Manny's

"Where you at, G?" asks
Manny. "I'm talking to you
and you're spacing." "What?
Oh. I'm just thinking about
this virus thing. Co-something."

"COVID? I call it
The Invisible Beast, but
some folks here say it's
no worse than the flu. I don't
know anyone with it. You?"

I shake my head. "Then
why you tripping, G? Don't go
borrowing trouble."
Like always, Manny's words help
settle me. "You good?" *I'm good*.

ATTENTION!

One night, Dad comes home
with a stack of face masks he
got from work. "You go
anywhere, you wear these. Clear?"
His glare wipes away my smile.

"They're disposable.
Use one, and toss it. Got it?"
I nod silently.
This Dad's no one to mess with.
This Dad's a little scary.

I guess he sees that
in my eyes because then he
gives me the longest
hug in history, I swear.
"It's okay, Dad. It's okay."

Phone Call Invitation

"G, are you hungry?"
Manny only asks if he's
whipping up dinner.
Kid or not, he's a great chef
so I say, "Be right over!"

I have never tried
veal marsala, but I'm sure
it's God's favorite dish.
I'm almost done making it
disappear when the world stops.

MARCH 19

Mom telephones me
with the news. "Come home," she says,
her voice taut as rope.
"I need you to help me shop.
California's on lockdown."

LOCK WHAT?

Our governor says
beginning tonight, our state
is hitting the switch,
shutting down everyday life
until further notice. What?

No work, no school, no
chorus, no baseball with Joe,
no meals with Manny,
no out, only in, except
for stocking up on supplies

till this storm passes.
At least it's warm enough here
in California
to hang out in the backyard
if indoors gets boring, but

how long will this be?
Three weeks? Four? Mom's not sure. "We'll
get back to normal.
Trust me. Not even the worst
hurricane can last for long."

AISLE FIVE

The Food Mart is filled
with a stampede of shoppers
trampling each other
for—toilet paper? This is
crazy! Get me out of here!

Back home, Angie helps
unpack the groceries while
Mom and Dad smuggle
dark whispers upstairs, as if
their worry has no echo.

Angie and I share
the truth with one long look: *This
Invisible Beast
must be worse than we thought.* But
we don't dare say it out loud.

New Day

The sun wakes me to
a day with nothing to do.
Angie's still asleep,
Dad's at work, and Mom's cramming
courses in online teaching.

The whole day feels like
an avalanche of questions:
When? What? Where? Why? And
how long will the lockdown last?
Does anyone even know?

What about chorus?
And when can I see my friends?
Joe says we can play
video games online and
chat on the phone, not that it's

exactly the same,
plus Manny's not into tech.
He likes books better.
Me, too. Don't know what I'll do
except play guitar, and read.

And what about Dad?
He has to keep installing
Wi-Fi in strange homes
so he still gets to go out.
Does that seem fair? I don't know.

Too many questions.
Yesterday, the only thing
I wanted to know
was "What's for dinner, Manny?"
When can we go back to that?

NEW SONG

I spend half the day
working on my fingering,
nailing three new chords
on my six-string. I can't wait
to show Dad when he gets home.

He opens the door
and I run, guitar in hand.
"Stop!" he yells. "Stay back!
Let me bag this uniform,
shower, and change clothes. Okay?"

I freeze, feel the fear
twist my insides. Is this how
it's going to be
from now until—whenever?
I back away, the song—gone.

55-Degree Shuffle

I roll out of bed
grab my mitt out of habit
and head downstairs. I'm
at the front door before it
hits me: no more meeting Joe

for our daily game
of catch. No more head slaps, no
noogies, no high fives.
It's too cold, anyway. I
might as well go back to bed.

GET PACKING

Sitting in Mom's car
I fidget with my mask. *Gah!*
Somebody give me
something to do, already!
It's two weeks since schools closed and

Mom's school scheduled time
for her to grab her whiteboard,
files, and whatever
else she needs to keep teaching
from home. What's crazy is they

won't let me help her.
Only teachers are allowed
to go inside. She
said that they didn't even
want teachers hanging around

chatting. Just sign in,
pack, and leave, lugging textbooks
and equipment through
the parking lot on your own.
Sheesh! I finally see Mom

trudging over. I
rush to open the trunk to
make her life easy.
Once everything's loaded, she
says, "You're great company." Right.

Beware the Ides of March 24th

Wait! What? This guy on
the news is saying some kid
in L.A. just died
from this new virus, and he
was not much older than me!

Suddenly, the earth
is cracking under my feet.
It's probably a
freak thing, Manny would say. *Why*
get all hyped up? So, I breathe.

RIPPLES

The next day, I hear
the sewing machine going
in Mom's room, but Mom's
downstairs. It's Angie with her
foot on the pedal. "Since when

do you sew?" I ask
ducking in the doorway. "Since
now. I've got masks to
make. Go!" *Message received. Bet
she saw that news report, too.*

SINGER SEWING

Angie becomes the
sewing queen, stitching seams and
bits of elastic
making masks every day. Like
she's so special. Whatever.

MEAN CLEAN

The kitchen smells like
a Lysol bomb exploded.
Call it overkill,
but Mom's at war, making sure
no deadly virus survives.

Hand-Washing Drill

"Sing 'Row, Row, Row Your
Boat,'" drills Sergeant Mom telling
me how long to wash
my hands—as if I haven't
washed them fifty thousand times!

CHECKING IN WITH MANNY

wyd
food science hbu
just reading mostly
We text about nothing, the
last normal thing left to do.

FIRST DAY BACK TO SCHOOL, SORT OF

I click Video
On, then jump back seeing my
face pop up in this
tiny square right next to a
kid who hardly ever speaks

to me in class. Now
here he is, in my bedroom.
Weird. I click off the
video. "I know this feels
strange," says the teacher. *You think?*

"But you need to keep
your cameras on until
I take attendance."
Whatever. Let's just get this
over—attendance, the first

day, the whole thing. K?
Some kids are missing. Lucky
them! Mom would never
let me get away with that.
So I'm stuck. Here. In Weird Land.

April Fools'

Godzilla's not real
but other monsters stomp in
during dinnertime
when Mom talks about COVID
rampaging round the planet.

"I hate this lockdown!
England, Australia, Japan—
teachers everywhere
are scrambling to master apps
and online teaching platforms.

The whole world's a mess."
"Pass the rice, please," I ask just
to change the subject.
Tired of hearing we're all in
the same boat, since it's sinking.

Hide-and-Seek

The Invisible
Beast chases me and I run
but I'm too slow, and
it steals my breath until—no!
I scream, waking in a sweat.

Social Distance

Finally, math is
good for something other than
taking tests. Only
now it's worse: I'm told to stay
six feet away from my friends.

Priority Bummer

Mom stuffs a padded
envelope with masks Angie
made, and puts them in the mail
for their journey to
our aunts, uncles, and cousins.

The government can't
make up its mind, but Mom's sure
wearing masks can help
keep family safe. I won't
argue, but it's a bummer.

I finally love
all of me. Now I'm told to
muzzle my nose and
the lips through which the music
inside me breaks free. Not. Fair.

BANDIT?

Shopping with Mom, a
kid says, "That mask makes you look
like a bank robber."
I freeze, hoping there is no
trigger-happy cop nearby.

Is he serious?
Or trying to be funny?
Which? When your skin's black,
those are not words to laugh at,
not when your parents teach you

to spend your life with
one eye over your shoulder,
looking for police
you'd better speak calmly to
so they don't shoot you on sight.

BACK HOME

I rip off my mask—
two months into lockdown—and
glare at Mom, thinking
Remember how you said we'd
get back to normal? When? WHEN?

CLEANING

Cleaning used to be
shirts, jeans, and underwear. Now
we have to wipe down
groceries and packages
from the post office. What's next?

CABIN FEVER

Angie laces up
for a quick run. "Can I come?"
Her mouth forms a no,
then changes. "Okay." Thank God!
My poor lungs scream for fresh air.

Two blocks and Angie
streaks ahead. No big surprise.
It's fine, though. I know
my way through the neighborhood.
I drink in sun and silence.

Home's so noisy now—
teachers blaring over Zoom,
Angie's screams when she
creams a video-game foe,
Mom cursing at teaching apps

she can't understand—
it's wild twenty-four seven.
If I want to read,
I need headphones. Who knew *out*
would become better than *in*?

NONSTOP

Daily virus death
reports blare from the TV
making me want to
smash that screen to smithereens.
Death. Death. Death! Stop already!

ONE BRIGHT NOTE

"God bless our district,"
Mom tells us over dinner.
"Since our schools closed down,
they set up a lunch program
for all households with children

eighteen or younger.
Principals, custodians,
and lunch ladies wait
outside of their schools in heat,
rain, and wind for two or three

hours every day
so families can drive up
and collect lunches
for their babies." A tear slides
down Mom's cheek as she speaks. Her

words unclog my throat,
untie the knots inside me.
It's hard not to choke
on your own food when you know
someone else is missing theirs.

MISSING IN ACTION

My lonely guitar
grows dusty waiting for me
to play or practice
but Dad's always too busy
for our lessons and duets.

He blames overtime.
"Lots of people need me to
set up their Wi-Fi,"
Dad explains, as if I care,
as if I don't need him, too.

EMPLOYED

Dad is out the door
before I can say goodbye.
Wish he was home more,
but we're lucky. Some kids' folks
no longer have jobs at all.

COMFORT

A few times a day
I turn up in the kitchen
hungry for something
to chew on besides worry,
thirsty for back-to-normal.

Pre-algebra

Sleep shading my eyes,
I jump on the computer
mumbling good morning
to my teacher, pretending
this is almost like real school.

Who am I kidding?
Math was always hard, but now
it's impossible!
Where's that raise-your-hand icon
you click to ask questions??? *Grrrr!*

After class, I run
downstairs for soda, dart past
Mom distance-teaching.
Her scowl sends a secret code.
I get the message. "Sorry!"

I tiptoe upstairs,
fizzy contraband in hand,
leaving Mom in peace.
Besides—gag—it's now time for
History, minus Black me.

SCALES

No chorus for now.
Even so, I practice scales
Do, re, mi, fa, so
just in case my voice and I
are invited out to play.

LOSING CONNECTION

I knock on Dad's door
for the second time this week.
He eyes my guitar,
strums my hope like strings, and says,
"Sorry. Maybe tomorrow."

Tomorrow. A word
that scrapes my ear till it bleeds.
Who needs more sour notes?
I'm tired of "Not tonight, Son."
Silent strings sing a sad song.

EVAPORATION

"So, when will my school
open again?" I ask Mom.
"I don't know, honey,"
she says. "A few weeks, maybe."
Apparently, she's wrong 'cause

weeks evaporate
while I wait for this lockdown
to end so I can
go back to school, to chorus,
to normal, to life before

but *before* seems like
something imaginary,
a wild fairy tale,
a dream I half remember,
one that is slipping away.

TTYL

My phone beeps. *knock knock*
It's Joe. Big surprise. *yo man*
wyd
me: *i'm playing No Man's Sky*
boring hmu later

I smile, figuring
Joe's got *Minecraft* on the brain,
his favorite game since
baseball went on lockdown like—
everything. There goes my smile.

SCHOOL DAY

Mom pops in and out
checking up on me between
teaching her own class,
like I'm some little kid who
can't seem to pay attention!

Yeah, it's different.
Sometimes the screen is a sea
my eyes swim in and
I get lost for a while, but
I wake up again. Mostly.

"You're a good student,
Garvey," Mom tells me. "That's why
I check in on you.
I want you to stay that way."
I shrug, thinking *Whatever*.

SHADOW

Deep into the new
Star Trek novel, a creaking
floorboard at my door
shatters my concentration.
It's Angie, who's allergic

to knocking. She stares
at me. "What?" I ask, annoyed.
Angie shrugs. "Nothing."
But her nothing doesn't go
away, and neither does she.

Catlike, she curls up
across the foot of my bed.
"What are you reading?"
"Why?" I can't remember when
Angie was interested

in books, unless they
were for homework, so what's up?
Angie purrs. "Could you
read me a few pages?" Now
I know the world is ending.

Life's a Beach

Me: "Did you hear this?
In Huntington Beach, thousands
hit the streets, swinging
picket signs 'cause the Gov closed
the beaches, for a minute.

I get that people
like to swim, but why risk it?"
Manny: "You tell me
there are sharks in the water,
I'm not going. You tell me

COVID's on that beach,
guess who you won't find in the
sand?" We both fist bump
our computer screens. *Lockdown's
making everyone crazy.*

RACE

Dad and I go get
groceries. "Let's give your mom
a break," he says. Fine.
But why turn it into a
race? I can barely keep up

chasing him from aisle
to aisle, making the cart fly
off its wheels. "Hurry!"
he calls over his shoulder.
"Run! Meet me at checkout." *Sheesh!*

MURDER HORNETS

Killer bees came first.
Now it's murder hornets? Wow.
What is happening?
Pandemics, police shootings,
monster bugs—give us a break!

VIRTUALLY SPEAKING

Sunday morning is
the wrong kind of quiet. Mom
and Dad sit in the
glow of their laptop, straining
to hear our Pastor Mike preach.

Angie sleeps in while
I fidget on the sofa
missing the blanket
of usual voices that
wrap us together in song.

Sure, worship music
plays in the background while Mom
mouths the words, but that
doesn't fill me like singing
out loud with others at church.

TABLE TALK

"Malcolm, did you hear?"
Mom asks Dad. "Some nurses are
threatening to strike
because they're working without
enough medical-grade masks."

"Well, you can't blame them,"
says Dad. Nobody asks me
but I'm thinking, *Then
who'll take care of sick people?
Isn't that what nurses do?*

I stay silent, though.
To ask or know any more
is just too scary.
"May I be excused?" For once,
I leave without an answer.

DAD: THE IT GUY COMES HOME

Dad checks our Wi-Fi,
which cut out twice this morning.
"Gah! Just what I need!"
Dad groans. Guess we're not working
on any new songs tonight.

GOOGLE SHEETS

I rub my eyes while
Mom rechecks my Google Sheets.
"It's all done," I say
between yawns. I notice dark
circles under Mom's eyes. "Mom,

you should go to sleep."
Love tugs the corners of her
mouth into a smile.
"In a minute, Son." I fling
my arms around her and squeeze,

then use one word to
push her toward the door. "Go!"
Finally, she leaves,
a mom older, slower than
I remember from before.

When COVID's over,
will I get my young mom back?
Will Dad and I play
music again? Ugh! I've got
to stop drowning in questions!

BALLOT BOX

I walk in the room
just in time to hear Mom say
"Looks like we all get
to vote by mail this year." I
shrug. The election was sure

more interesting
when Kamala was in it.
Now, it's back to the
usual: one old white man
versus another. Boring.

Comic Relief

Angie and I see
how tired Mom is getting. "I'll
make dinner tonight,"
says Angie. "Garvey will help."
I give her the side-eye, but

now I can't refuse
without looking bad, and she
knows it. I growl and
wait for instructions. "Let's see . . .
I know! How about tacos?"

Yum, I think—until
it's clear which one of us will
do all the chopping:
tomatoes, avocadoes,
onions. Ugh! In two minutes

the tears are running.
"Quit crying," says Angie. "And
don't touch your eyes! Wash
your hands, then shred the lettuce
and the cheese." "*Dang!*" I say. "And

what exactly are
you doing? 'Cause it feels like
I'm the one cooking."
Angie browns ground turkey and
pays me no mind. *Oh, really?*

I fling bits of cheese
in her direction. She blinks,
then says, "Oh, it's on!"
She grabs shredded lettuce and
I duck, squealing as food flies

across the kitchen.
"What is going on in there?"
asks Mom. Sis and I
choke on laughter. "Nothing!" we
say, loving the way we feel.

FaceTime

Manny hates FaceTime,
which tells me something is up.
His wet eyes warn me
the news is not good. I gulp.
"My grandma's got COVID, G."

What's worse than bad? *This.*
"Sorry, man. Is she . . . okay?"
That sounds so lame, but
what else can I say? I mean
I can't ask if she's dying.

"She's coughing real bad,"
Manny says, "so she's staying
in her room, for now."
For now—two words that echo.
I hope out loud. "She'll be fine."

"Thanks, G," says Manny.
Meanwhile, funeral scenes float
up into my mind,
but I shake them away, tell
both of us she'll be okay.

THE INVISIBLE BEAST

Epidemic, plague,
scourge, pestilence—whichever
fancy word you choose—
this pandemic is proving
to be the worst kind of news.

Angie's Joy

The basketball hoop
hanging in our driveway keeps
Angie busy. I'd
be jealous, but this virus
sent her hoop-joy out of bounds.

GARVEY'S BIRTHDAY

"Drive-by? Virtual?
What will it be?" Mom asks me.
As if it matters,
as if COVID doesn't make
this year's birthday just feel fake.

GIFT

For my birthday, Sis
drives me to the mountains where
we can walk mask-less
and stick closer than six feet
and no one is there to care.

HOSPITAL EMERGENCY

I'm beginning to
hate the word *ventilator.*
Each letter marches
one step closer to death. But
I keep that thought to myself

since Manny's grandma
is on one. The hospital
signed her in last night.
Manny couldn't follow, but
his prayers tiptoed in unseen.

Broadcast

TV anchors say
hospitals are filling up.
Thousands of people
sick and dying every day.
I wish Mom would stop watching.

Cough

This morning, Dad coughs.
It's probably nothing, right?
Just a normal cold.
Or no. Worry grabs my gut
strangling me from the inside.

Breathe, I tell myself,
then I text Joe, next Manny.
Joe: *dw chill*
Manny: *sry fx*
Fingers crossed, I chill—and pray.

Fitness Freak

I go looking for
a book Angie borrowed. What
I find instead are
chips littering her bed. Since
when does Angie eat junk food?

LOST AND FOUND

The basketball net
blows lonely in the wind, no
Angie shooting hoops
to give it purpose. She says
it's just no fun without Dad

or friends to play with.
Her eyes are dull as old dimes,
which I can't stand so
here goes: "Sis, could you teach me
how to do a layup shot?"

ANGIE'S TURN

I knock on Mom's door.
"Yes! I'm Angie's mom," she says
into her phone. *Sigh*.
I'd have to be a teacher
to get her attention now.

SLEEPLESS

One night, Dad's coughing
rumbles through the halls and walls,
a train off its track.
His hack's not the only thing
that keeps me awake for hours.

NOWHERE TO HIDE

Test results today
make it official: no more
work for Dad. COVID
has him in a choke hold. Now
I'm finding it hard to breathe.

PANDEMIC MULTIPLICATION

The six o'clock news
makes me retch. COVID deaths pass
too many thousands.
No one likes that kind of math,
especially in this house.

WHAT IF, WHAT

What if, what if, what—
I can't stop thinking about
what might happen if
my dad has to go into
the hospital, but there are

no beds, or what if
the nurses are on strike, or
the ventilators
run out, or there's not enough
medicine, or, or, or—God!

I wish my brain would
just shut up already! Please!
Dad will be fine. He
says he'll be fine. Mom says he'll
be fine. Not to worry. Right.

CONVERSATION

"No hospital, Grace,"
I hear Dad instruct Mom. "They
have too few beds and
ventilators, anyway."
I think of Manny's grandma

in that hospital
cut off from all visitors
and gulp. *God, promise*
you'll let Dad stay here at home
with his family. With me.

QUARANTINE

How do you spell fear?
I'd rather go back to Dad
always being tired,
which is better than sick. Now
both of us are shivering,

Dad with his fever,
me with this awful knowing
that my dad could—*No!*
I can't go there. Much better
to hide inside of a book.

Off-Limits

The virus sends Dad
into the guest room as if
he's a visitor.
Sometimes, I press my ear to
the door, just to hear him breathe.

It's hard to believe
my own dad is off-limits
like he's the disease
instead of just having it.
"Hang in there, Dad," I whisper.

GOOD NEWS

I get a text from
Manny telling me his gram
is getting better.
She's off the ventilator.
Great! But what about my dad?

SPECIAL DELIVERY

We're prisoners! We
can't even go shopping now!
Our groceries have
to be delivered. Dad's not
the only one quarantined.

FRESH AIR

Is there any left,
anywhere? Air that's not been
poisoned by COVID?
Some days, I run to the yard
and take a deep breath to check.

And it's not just me.
I find Angie out there, too,
kicking around her
soccer ball, sprinting, boxing
her shadow—anything to

test her lungs, I guess.
With Dad sick, I think we're both
checking our bodies
to see if they're still working,
to see if we're still okay.

HOME NURSE

Mom puts on her mask
and carries a tray of food
upstairs to the room
holding Dad as prisoner.
Her mask almost hides her tears.

Book Two on Order

Angie pads into
my room, desperate for our
nightly reading. Well,
I read. She listens. "What's up
for tonight?" she asks, curling

catlike in my chair.
*"Tristan Strong Punches a Hole
in the Sky."* I've read
it before, but I don't mind.
I kind of like sharing it

with Angie. Besides,
Book Two won't be out for months.
Right now, we both need
something to take our minds off
of—you know. So, "Chapter One."

TALK IT OUT

I chat with Manny
on FaceTime for as many
hours as it takes me
to breathe again. It's strange how
worry sucks up all the air.

"You look awful, G."
Manny never minces words.
I follow his lead.
"Dad's got it and now we're all
on quarantine. It's scary."

The last word stumbles
on its journey to my mouth,
but I spit it out.
Manny's eyes say, *Sorry. I
know how you feel.* And he does.

Itchy Feet

Some pastors vote to
reopen churches, but I'm
with Pastor Mike who
says, "We're in no hurry. God
can bless us just fine online."

REFUGE

My room a haven,
I lose myself in *Tight*, a
novel with a boy
quiet as me. *Bryan, please
take me away for a while.*

ESSENTIAL

I remember when
I thought Dad was so lucky
being essential.
Now I know that mostly means
you get to risk getting sick.

Tell me how that's fair!
Nobody cares about him,
about us, or me.
What am I supposed to do
if he never gets better?

It's Complicated

Manny's grandmother
finally gets to go home.
I'm happy for him
but jealous, too. That's kind of
messed up, but what can I do?

WITNESS

Joe texts me a link
to a video. *yo you
gotta see this*, he
tells me. He's right, though a few
minutes in, I'm screaming *No!*

Tic, Tic, Tic

Rage ripples through me
as a white man, cold as stone,
calmly steals the breath
of a man black as me by
pinning him to the ground and

kneeling on his neck
as the minutes tic, tic, tic
and George Floyd whispers
for his mom and the missing
mercy hiding where? And why?

Going Numb

I can't feel my fists,
my feet, the tears on my cheek,
only disbelief
'cause this policeman couldn't
care less that the world's watching.

FLOYD'S FINAL BREATH

The house too quiet,
Mom leaves the kitchen, finds me
and sees what I see.
"Lord! No!" she cries, arriving
too late to cover my eyes.

After

Someone has just died.
Dinner is a funeral.
It doesn't matter
that George Floyd is a stranger.
Our black skin makes us all kin.

NOTHING TO SAY

"This is whack!" says Joe
when we chat online. "No one
should have to go out
like that, yo, begging to breathe."
My anger and I simmer.

PROTESTS

No justice, no peace
runs on a loop through my mind
and I'm supposed to
focus on school? History
is happening in the streets

and I can't go! "We're
still on quarantine," Mom says.
Like I could forget!
"None of us can take chances
of getting sick ourselves or

spreading this virus.
Plus it's not safe to march, Son."
Isn't that the point?
When you're Black, you're never safe.
Just ask George Floyd. Wait! You can't.

I Get It

I get why Mom's scared.
Police are shooting rubber
bullets, and they shoved
a seventy-five-year-old
man to the ground so hard he

cracked his skull. Mom thinks
that could have been me, but I
move faster than an
old man. Still, I might not be
quicker than rubber bullets.

"Maybe, when your dad's
better, we can all go march
together, as a
family. That way we can
look out for each other." *Deal.*

Countdown to Summer Break

For the next few days,
I switch on my computer,
half mad, half buried
in worry about my dad.
I'm glad school's almost over.

LOST IN SPACE

Sis and I need to
lose ourselves inside of a
movie. But which one?
"Easy," I say. "*Star Wars: The
Rise of Skywalker!*" Angie

groans. "Sci-fi? Again?"
"But wait!" I argue, "You love
strong women, right?" I
pull up the trailer. "Fine," she
says. *Yes!* "But next time, I choose."

SNEAK

I open Dad's door
softly so Mom won't catch me.
"Dad? It's me, Garvey."
He's too weak to even turn
towards me. I step closer

and rip my mask off
so my voice won't sound muffled.
But next thing I know,
bear claws are gripping my wrist,
yanking me out of that room.

Mom must have slipped in
on tiptoe, silent as snow.
"What were you thinking?"
She trembles, more scared than mad.
"You know you can't go in there!"

"Sorry," I whisper.
Mom suffocates her fear by
squeezing me so hard
my bones groan. "Be. More. Careful,"
she says. "Promise me!" I nod.

FULL STEAM

Is the world on fire?
There are protests in France, Spain,
Kenya, Korea—folks in
sixty countries believing
Black lives matter! Dad's sure does.

DONE!

Goodbye, Google Meets.
Later, Flipgrids and Zoom rooms!
Adios, homework!
I've got more important things
on my mind at the moment.

PEACEFUL PROTEST

Every time I hear
the words *riot* and *protest*
slapped together, it
makes me want to spit. They are
not the same! Protesters are

not to blame for what
a few rioters do, but
does anyone care?
Nothing about racism
is fair, or right, or past tense.

GREAT ESCAPE

Manny's like me. He
can't join the protests, either.
He needs to stay home
to help care for his grandma
until she recovers. But

meanwhile, we both seethe
about Breonna Taylor,
George Floyd, and way too
many others. We group-watch
Black Panther about a world

in which our people
have value and *justice* is
a word everyone
can spell. In unison, we
yell, "WAKANDA FOREVER!"

JEALOUS

"You should have been there!"
says Joe, just coming back from
a local protest.
"Marching with all those people
to get justice for George Floyd

made me feel strong, like
I was *doing* something, right?"
I clench my fist, but
jealousy will have to wait
till COVID cuts my dad loose.

I don't want to leave
him till then. Besides, Mom says
the protests will still
be there. "Sadly, injustice
isn't going anywhere."

JUNE GLOOM

"Why. Don't. People. Get.
That. Black. Lives. Matter???" Angie
pounds her words like nails,
sharp tips puncturing the air.
She's not waiting for answers

I don't have. For once,
we are both mad together.
"I joined a protest,"
she confesses. My eyes swell.
"Wow!" I promise not to tell.

After-Dinner Whispers

Angie and I clear
the table. "Garvey, I think
Dad's getting worse." We
share our fears, till Mom appears.
"What's up, guys?" "Nothing!" we lie.

DOWNHILL

"Please. Eat something. Try!"
I hear Mom pleading with Dad.
"Can't. Go," he wheezes.
From my door, I watch her leave
his room with the dinner tray

of hardly eaten
soup and crackers. This is the
third day in a row.
Sis thinks Dad's discouraged. If
he doesn't eat soon, he'll—*No!*

I can't let Dad go.
But what can I do? Think. Think!
Wait. There was something
Dad once said. "Your voice could wake
the dead." I grab my guitar

run to his room and
open his door just a crack.
Help me, Lord. I find
the right chords and start singing
my favorite song, and Dad's too.

Song Interrupted

By the second verse
I hear Dad's voice, weak, but there
trying to chime in!
"No!" Mom comes running. "Leave! Now!"
But Dad croaks, "Let the boy be."

He takes a long breath.
"Garvey's helping me. Sing, Son."
Mom gasps with surprise
when Dad tries to sing too. His
voice grows stronger with each note,

hope filling the room,
filling me. Could Dad really
start to get better?
Eyes closed, I keep singing "Dance
with My Father" like a prayer.

THERMOMETER

"How's Dad today?" I
ask, afraid of the answer.
Maybe I only
imagine he'll start to get
better. "His fever broke," says

Mom. I almost choke
on hope. "Really?" I check to
make sure I heard right.
"Really," says Mom, and the drum
of my heart slows its beat. *Ahhh!*

THE RUNS

Mom stops hogging the
bathroom Angie and I share
now that Dad doesn't
get the runs as often as
he had been since you-know-who

came for a visit.
Let's just say everybody's
glad to have their own
bathrooms back, not to mention
there's less flushing going on.

THE RETURN OF QUIET

I toss in the night,
restless in the quiet. What's
missing? I strain for
the answer. Dad's cough! I don't
hear it and haven't for hours!

I throw back the sheets
and sit up. *Wait!* It hits me:
The Invisible
Beast is in retreat! I can
finally hear sleep calling.

END OF QUARANTINE

Dad's contagion has
passed now. No more quarantine!
I can't wait to tell
Joe and Manny. I spill it
in a group chat. "Great!" says Joe.

"Glad he didn't need
the hospital like my Gram,"
says Manny. "You know,
I keep thinking about the
people still in there, feeling

alone and scared, G.
And the nurses and doctors
worn out from trying
to heal hundreds of people.
Wish we could help them somehow."

A new idea
mushrooms inside me. "I know!
A concert, Manny!
A bunch of us could go and
sing outside the hospital,

lift people's spirits!
Why not?" Manny starts to glow.
"That sounds dope!" says Joe.
"We'll need some sound equipment."
"And more voices!" says Manny.

"I'll send out a text.
I'll bet some kids from chorus
will want to join us."
Something warm and familiar
starts to ripple through us—joy?

DETAILS

Joe's aunt, a nurse, hooks
us up with the hospital.
They set up links for
our performance so patients
can see and hear it right on

the TVs in their
own rooms. You know what that means?
Even the sickest
patients get to hear us sing!
I just need Mom's permission!

I rehearse: *Of course,*
we'll all be standing six feet
apart. Yes, we'll be
outside the whole time. No, we
won't get in the doctors' way.

Yes, opposite the
main entrance, which is deep as
three sequoia trees!
Well, practically. Yes, I'd call
that a safe distance away.

Gah! What do you think
the sound equipment is for?
Wait. I better not
say anything like that or
else I'll never get to go.

Okay. Let's do this.
"Mom? Do you have a minute?"
I lay out the plan,
mention Manny, the other
kids from chorus, even Joe.

Joe's no singer, but
who can't use an extra friend?
Mom's quick to agree.
"Just steer clear of protests—for
now," she warns. *Whew! That went well.*

CONCERT

I'm feeling nauseous.
Soon folks will be watching from
nurse station TVs,
cafeterias, lounges,
and maybe from windows, right?

But nobody said
I should probably expect
dozens of nurses
and doctors in the entry—
hungry eyes staring at me.

"Ready?" asks Manny.
I nod and take a deep breath,
grateful that I can.
Then I lower my mask and
sing as if God's listening.

WEIGHT LOSS

No part of me wants
to be sick, but I can't help
noticing that Dad
came out of the quarantine
room smaller than he went in.

Appetite in Sight

Tonight, Dad hobbles
to the dinner table, his
energy half what
it used to be. Still, he beats
me to the last fish taco!

Over dinner, I
blurt out the wonders of the
day, tell Dad about
the concert, then I swim in
the pride spilling from his eyes.

MAIL CALL

I volunteer to
check the mailbox at our curb.
Any excuse to
go outside, these days, is a
good one, not that I expect

any mail for me.
What? There's something with my name
on it. Two rips and
I'm in. "Dear Garvey," it reads,
"I'm writing on behalf of

the hospital staff . . ."
A thank-you card! For me! Well,
for all of us who
put on that concert. Wow. I
read the card again, greedy

for every morsel
of praise. I chew on "spirits
lifted," on "soulful,"
on "staff and patients needed
that more than you'll ever know."

Eventually,
I glide back inside, no wings
required. "What took
so long?" asks Mom. "Nothing," I
say, tucking the card away.

I want this Oh-Wow!
feeling all to myself for
a minute. Then I'll
text the guys, show the card to
Mom and—*Dang! Why's my cheek wet?*

GETTING SOME AIR

Step by step, I guide
Dad to the end of the block.
"Hold up, Son," he says,
huffing. "Let me catch my breath."
"Sure, Dad," I say, slowing my

stride. For once, I'm the
hare and he's the tortoise. Weird.
My regular Dad
walks so fast, he has to wait
for me. When will he be back?

BETTER DAYS

The basketball smacks
the curb out front. I figure
it's Angie dribbling
the ball, till I look out and
see Dad! He's still moving slow,

but he's moving. Sis
joins him. "Come on, Old Man," she
says. "Let's play some one
on one." Dad chuckles. "You're on!"
Angie lets him win, this once.

STROLL

Family walks are
a thing now. Angie and me
lead the way. Today
we link our arms together.
We never did that before.

Tough Talk

"Your Mom tells me you
wanted to join the protests
after the killing
of George Floyd. Sorry that you
missed it." "Yeah, well." I just shrug.

There were a few big
rallies in L.A., even
in Hollywood, but
then the city set curfews
and after Floyd's funeral

the protests pretty
much faded away. At least
for now. So. "You know,"
says Dad, "protests aren't the end.
Black lives don't stop mattering,

Son. Marching's not the
only way to let folks know
our lives matter, too.
We can show the world that each
day in how we live, what we

say, the dignity
we carry ourselves with, and
the respect we show
one another. Then, when there
are protests again, we'll go."

I bite my lips to
keep my feelings tucked inside
then strangle Dad in
a hug that nearly cuts off
his breathing. *I love you, Dad.*

MEAT ON HIS BONES

Out of habit, I
give Dad the once-over and
notice he looks less
like a slice of who he was,
and more like his solid self.

He's back to giving
me guitar lessons again.
We duet our way
through July, breathing mask-less
and easy out in the yard.

Mom says the county's
still voting on what day in
August school should start,
so I don't need to worry
about that, yet. Suits me fine.

I want as many
lazy days with Dad as I
can possibly squeeze
in this summer. After all,
we've got months to make up for.

TANKA

Tanka is an ancient poetry form, originally from Japan. The word *tanka* means "short poem" in Japanese. The basic tanka is five lines long. The line-by-line syllable count varies in the modern English version, but the number of lines is always the same.

The modern form of tanka I chose to use for *Garvey in the Dark* is broken down as follows:

Line 1: 5 syllables
Line 2: 7 syllables
Line 3: 5 syllables
Line 4: 7 syllables
Line 5: 7 syllables.

Not every American poet follows a syllable count for tanka poems, but I think of a syllable count like a puzzle. Each word is a puzzle piece, and I like figuring out which words fit best!

Traditional tanka poems focus on mood. They are often poems about love, the four seasons, the shortness of life, and nature. In my tanka, I include mood, but in each poem, my focus is more centered on telling a story.

I hope you enjoyed the stories I told!

ACKNOWLEDGMENTS

There never seems to be enough space to name all of the people who touch a book during its journey, but I have to try.

It took a village to paint a picture for me of a teacher's experience of distance teaching during the pandemic. Countless numbers of you generously answered the questions I posted on social media, and I send hugs to each of you. You know who you are!

Special thanks to the teachers I returned to, again and again, with seemingly endless questions about in-home classroom setups, online teaching programs, teaching materials, and more. Lori Lopez, Beth West, Ashley Lemen, and Paige Tunie, I could not have written this novel without you!

To understand the impact of the pandemic on the sibling dynamic, I went to several parents for help. Thank you, Tricia Elisara, Judy Bailey, and Elizabeth Harding for your thoughtful, in-depth responses to my inquiries.

What do I know about hospital systems, or how a concert might be planned at such an institution, particularly during a pandemic? The answer is: exactly nothing, and so I turned to nurses Tracey Roeder and LaVerne Bennett, and hospital-based therapist Jennifer Larratt-Smith for input. A thousand thanks to you three!

A huge round of applause to Brent Roeder, as well, for his assist when the conversation turned to sound equipment, and what might work for my fictional concert.

I am one of those fortunate people who has, thus far, avoided exposure to COVID-19, so I'm grateful to Dan and Julie Weatherford for illuminating the experience of becoming ill with, and slowly recovering from COVID-19 so that I could more honestly reflect that experience in my story.

Big thanks to Brian Barnes for specifics on tech professions that helped me flesh out Garvey's dad and his essential work early on in the pandemic. You know how I love all things tech. Not!

Thanks, always, to my chief reader, Amy Malskeit. Your thoughtful critique did not disappoint!

Lastly, thanks to my editor, Rebecca Davis. This was a tough one, but you hung in there, and the novel is the beneficiary!

ENJOY MORE OF
GARVEY'S WORLD IN

GARVEY'S CHOICE

The more his dad wants him to be a jock, the more
Garvey tries to fill the hole in his heart with food.
Garvey has an important choice to make, one that could
be the key to getting everyone—including his father
and his taunting classmates—to see and accept the real
Garvey. . . .

Praise and honors for *Garvey's Choice*

A School Library Journal Best Book
A Kirkus Reviews Best Book
An ALSC Notable Children's Book
A YALSA Quick Pick for Reluctant Young Adult Readers

★ *Kirkus Reviews*, starred review
★ *School Library Journal*, starred review
★ *Publishers Weekly*, starred review
★ *Booklist*, starred review
★ *School Library Connection*, starred review

COMING SOON

GARVEY'S CHOICE
THE GRAPHIC NOVEL

By Nikki Grimes
Illustrated by Theodore Taylor III

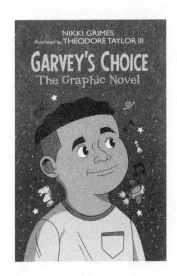

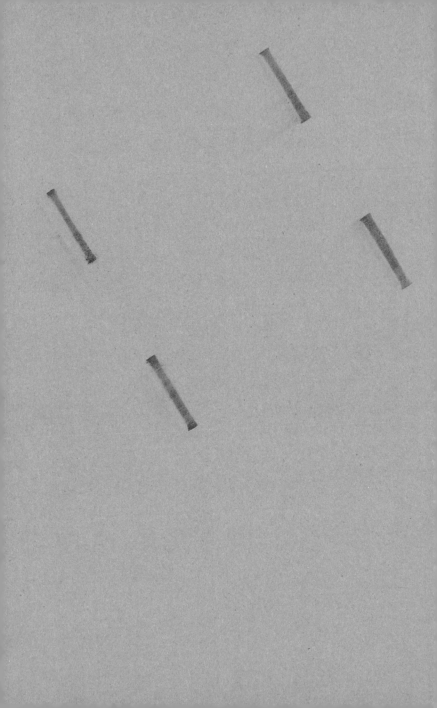